Campfire Tales

western adventures

by

Mark Phialas

Watermill Press

Printed in the United States of America

Illustrations by Jim Odbert

ISBN 0-89375-743-8

Contents

The Lost Mine

Ernest and Long Bill worked their way up the mountain. They had been here many times.

"We're just fools looking for fool's gold," Ernest had often said.

But Long Bill would just grin. "The Lost Mine is in this mountain," he would say with certainty. Then, he would give his old friend a shove. And they would go up the mountain one more time to try to find the Lost Mine.

"Let's try looking near that spring," Long Bill said.

"We did that yesterday," Ernest said.

"I've got an idea," said Long Bill. "Come on, Alonzo."

Alonzo was their mule. He could be very lazy. Sometimes, he would just sit down on the trail and not budge.

But today, Alonzo could smell the spring. And he was thirsty. So, Ernest and Long Bill made good time up the mountain.

When they got to the spring, Alonzo took a long drink. The men unpacked their equipment.

Long Bill walked to a large group of rocks by the spring. He took his pick and began to work. After a while, the

Long Bill took his pick and began to work.

pick lodged in the ground.

"I've hit some wood!" he cried, yanking the pick free. Then, he swung his pick again. Tiny bits of wood flew in the air.

Ernest ran over. This might be the entrance to the Lost Mine! How else could you explain wood in the middle of a rock pile?

Ernest and Long Bill used their picks for hours. They found a lot of wood in the ground.

"This is it!" Long Bill cried. The men worked harder. After years of looking for this lost mine, they had finally found it.

They dug deeper. Then, they came to a huge boulder.

"Alonzo will have to help with this," Long Bill said.

They tied a rope around the boulder.

Then, Long Bill tied the other end around Alonzo.

"Earn your dinner!" Long Bill cried. "Pull!"

But Alonzo did not budge. Long Bill tried to make Alonzo pull. But the mule stood his ground.

Then, Long Bill reached into his coat and found some rock candy. Alonzo was very fond of rock candy.

Long Bill waved the candy in front of Alonzo to tempt him. Then, he moved a few feet away from the mule.

"Do you want the candy?" he asked Alonzo. "Well, come and get it!"

Alonzo liked being lazy. But he was never lazy about candy.

It took just a few seconds for the mule to pull the boulder and reach the candy. Long Bill gave the candy to Alonzo. Then, he gave the mule an extra piece.

It took just a few seconds for the mule to pull the boulder.

The men were now able to push the boulder away.

And in front of them, a large, black hole fell away into darkness.

They just stared. This was the entrance to the Lost Mine!

"Now what?" asked Ernest.

"We get our lanterns, go into that mine, and get rich!" cried Long Bill.

"That sounds like a good idea," Ernest said.

Long Bill lit a lantern and peered into the entrance. "It's a mine, all right," he said. "I can see the support beams."

Ernest lit his lantern and raced to the entrance.

"Easy, partner," Long Bill warned. "We'd better take our time. We don't want this old mine to cave in."

"Right, right," agreed Ernest.

They worked carefully, moving rocks

away from the entrance. At last, there was room to get into the mine.

"Now?" asked Ernest.

"Now!" grinned Long Bill. And they walked into the entrance of the mine together.

The mine was damp and dusty. But they didn't care. After all, they were in the Lost Mine. Soon, they would be rich men!

They took their small picks and tapped the wall.

Long Bill stopped and held the lantern so that Ernest could see his work.

"I've got something!" Ernest cried. There was a dark object on the end of his pick.

Long Bill grabbed the dark object and held it in the light.

"It's a piece of coal!" said Long Bill.

"Coal?" Ernest asked.

Long Bill held the lantern so that Ernest could see.

Long Bill sadly nodded.

"The Lost Mine is a *coal* mine," Long Bill muttered.

"Maybe the gold is somewhere else in here?" Ernest asked.

Long Bill sat down with his head in his hands.

"There is no gold," he moaned. "All these years, we've been looking for a coal mine."

Ernest sat down next to his partner.

"You were right about one thing," he said.

"What's that?"

"The Lost Mine *is* in this mountain."

Long Bill looked at Ernest. Then, both of them began to laugh.

"Now what?" Long Bill finally asked.

"There's always another mountain," said Ernest. Long Bill nodded.

They left the mine and untied Alonzo.

Then, Ernest, Long Bill, and their mule hit the trail towards another dream.

And someday that dream might just come true.

The Red River Gang

Sheriff Ford pinned a badge on Jim Clark's vest.

"I'm mighty pleased you're my new deputy," Sheriff Ford said.

"Thanks," said Jim. "I hope I do all right."

"Just keep your eyes and ears open," the sheriff said.

Jim sat at his desk. He looked through

the pictures of outlaws. Then, he came to a picture of four men. They were called the Red River Gang. And they were wanted for robbery in five states.

"These guys get around," Jim said.

"But the Red River Gang hasn't come to Arizona," Sheriff Ford said. "I'm hoping they never do!"

Jim nodded his head. "I like things quiet myself," he said.

Just then, the sound of breaking glass pierced the air. *Crash!*

Jim grabbed his hat and put on his gun belt. The gun felt heavy on his thigh.

He walked into the street. Two men were arguing in front of the general store.

"What's going on?" Jim asked.

"Are you the law?" one of the men asked.

Two men were arguing in front of the general store.

"You guessed right," Jim said.

"This guy sold me flour with bugs in it!" the man shouted.

"Does that mean he should break my window?" the shop owner asked.

"You shouldn't sell bad flour," the first man said.

"How was I to know?" said the store owner.

"Hold it!" Jim shouted.

He told the men they could settle things two ways. They could both go to jail. Or they could agree on a plan at the store.

"You look like a nice guy," Jim said to the first man. "Pay him for his window."

Then, Jim turned to the shop owner. "Give him a bag of flour and credit for another bag when he needs it."

Jim said that everyone should be satisfied now.

The men agreed to do this. But the shop owner looked puzzled. "Say, are you new?" he asked Jim.

"Not anymore," Jim smiled.

About a week later, Sheriff Ford had to go to Phoenix.

"I'll be back in a few days," the sheriff said.

Jim felt a little uneasy. He would have to watch the town by himself.

Early the next morning, he was cleaning the windows in the jail. It was barely light outside, and the streets were empty.

Four men rode into town. They were dirty and tired. They looked like they had been riding all night.

Jim finished the windows and went back to his desk. Then, a picture flashed in his mind! *The Red River Gang!*

At first, Jim couldn't move. His hands were shaking.

Sheriff Ford had to go to Phoenix.

The Red River Gang was very dangerous. There were four of them, and only one of Jim! He grabbed his shotgun and went out the back door of the jail.

Jim turned the corner. The Red River Gang was in front of the bank. One of the outlaws kicked open the bank door. Then all of the men went inside.

Jim crossed the street. It was empty. The Red River Gang liked to do their robbing while people were asleep.

Jim crouched near the bank window. Inside, the outlaws were working on the safe with a hammer and a chisel.

I need some help, Jim thought. Then, he had an idea. The outlaws didn't know he was alone.

"Throw down your guns and come out with your hands up!" Jim yelled. "Sam and Harry, cover the back door! Watch the front window, Bill. The rest of you

One of the outlaws kicked open the bank door.

men, keep your guns pointed on the front door!"

It was a bluff, but it might work. Jim cocked his shotgun. Tiny beads of sweat rolled down his face.

Clump! Clump! Clump! Three pistols lay in the street.

Jim heard a voice inside the bank say, "It's over, Butch. Throw your gun down."

Clump!

The Red River Gang came out of the bank with their hands above their heads. Blinking from the glare of the rising sun, the outlaws were puzzled.

"Where's the mob?" one outlaw asked.

"Let's go," Jim said.

Two outlaws rushed towards Jim. Jim sidestepped the first man. And with the barrel of his shotgun, he knocked the other man to the street.

A third outlaw ran towards his horse, but stopped when Jim fired his gun into the air.

"Everyone freeze!" Jim commanded. "Now, lie face down, hands away from your sides."

Slowly, the outlaws obeyed.

Jim checked each man for hidden weapons. Satisfied, he ordered the men to stand.

"We're going to take a short walk to a large cell," Jim said. "We have reservations for four under the name of the Red River Gang."

Night of Fury

Jed Masters rode to the edge of the canyon. He surveyed his cattle and his trail crew. He had over a thousand head of the best cattle this side of Kansas City.

Jed was from Houston, Texas. He and his men were going to Kansas City, to sell the herd.

As Jed rode into camp, he felt a twinge of pain.

"My shoulder has been annoying me all day," he said. "I may be wrong, but I bet we're in for a storm."

Harry looked at Jed with a slight smile.

"It's clear as far as you can see," said Harry. "But maybe that isn't too far!"

Some of the other men laughed. Jed laughed, too.

"I must be getting old," he said. "All right, let's get moving."

A cattle drive is hard, dirty work. It had been very dry, and the air was thick with dust.

By sunset, they had traveled 15 miles. It had been a good day. And everybody was exhausted.

"We'll make camp here," Jed said. "Tomorrow, we'll head down to the valley."

The camp was near a steep cliff that looked over another valley.

Lightning streaked across the sky.

"I know it sounds crazy," said Jed. "But I want a double watch on the herd tonight."

"Whose turn is it?" asked Harry.

"It's mine," Amos said. "And you're up too, Harry!"

"Oh, brother!" Harry groaned.

Night watch is hard work. It means staying up after a full day of riding. Nobody liked night watch.

Amos and Harry took their places. At first, all was quiet and still.

But the wind began to grow stronger. This made the cattle a little uneasy.

Harry looked at the clouds forming in the sky. "Maybe Jed was right," he said. "We could be due for a storm."

By now, the winds grew stronger. Dust and sand whipped through the air.

Crack! Lightning streaked across the sky. Then, BOOM! Thunder rumbled in the air.

The loud noise scared the cattle. They began to get restless.

"They look like they're getting spooked," Amos said. "I'd better get help."

But he was too late.

Lightning and thunder crashed at the same time. Rain began to pour.

Crack! Boom!

A bolt of lightning hit the chuck wagon. The chuck wagon began to burn. Fire was rising high into the air!

The whole camp was now in motion. The men had only one thought. *Save the herd!*

Jed and the other men tried to saddle their horses. But they couldn't. The horses were wild with fear.

Crack! Boom!

Lightning hit close to the herd. The

cattle began to run. Soon, the entire herd was out of control, running towards the cliff.

Harry and Amos rode as hard as they could. They tried to turn the herd around. They rode near the cattle and waved their arms.

One of the steers banged into Harry's horse. Harry and his horse fell in front of the herd.

Harry screamed as the herd ran over him.

Amos looked back towards Harry. There was nothing Amos could do.

He drew his gun and fired into the air. He hoped this noise would frighten the cattle and turn them around.

The herd got closer and closer to the cliff.

Jed and the others came riding hard. They had their guns out, too.

Bang! Bang! Bang!

But nothing seemed to work.

Crack! Boom!

A bolt of lightning cracked in front of the lead steer. The lead steer turned to his right. The rest of the herd followed.

The herd had changed its direction! The rain stopped soon after that. And as the storm grew quiet, so did the herd.

Jed and his men gathered the cattle and returned to camp.

The cook had put out the fire on his chuck wagon. There had not been too much damage to the camp.

But Harry was dead.

Amos thought of Harry a long time. Wiping a tear, he bowed his head.

"He was a good man," Amos said. "He may have been a little lazy, but he always did his share of the work. He was

Harry was dead.

a nice man, a friend, and I'll miss him."

Amos grabbed a shovel from the chuck wagon and went to dig a grave.

Jed and his men had saved the herd. But they had lost their friend.

The Wagon Train

A wagon train moved slowly across the prairie. The people in the wagon train wanted to live in the west. And they were bringing all that they owned. The heavy wagons were each packed full.

Billy and Fred walked behind their wagon.

"How long until we get to California?" Fred asked.

A wagon train moved slowly across the prairie.

"You just asked me that!" cried Billy.

"How long?" Billy's younger brother asked again.

"I don't know!" Billy shouted. Fred was a year younger than Billy. And, sometimes, he could be a pain in the neck.

The two boys had been told to stay close to the wagons. They were safer that way.

But Billy wanted to be by himself. Fred was asking too many questions. *And besides,* Billy thought, *I can take care of myself.*

Billy saw a steep hill. He decided to climb it on his own. When he got to the top, he looked out as far as he could.

The land was rugged. The sky was clear. At the bottom of the hill was a meadow where a herd of buffalo grazed.

Beyond the meadow, Billy saw a

small stream. He decided he wanted a drink. So he walked around the edge of the herd. He was careful not to make any noise. He didn't want to disturb the buffalo.

When Billy got to the stream, he took a long drink. Then he took off his shoes and stuck his feet in the cool water.

"Wow! This feels great!" Billy said to himself.

After a while, it was time to head back to the wagons. He put his shoes on and started back up the hill.

Just then, Fred came running towards him.

"Hey, Billy!" he shouted. "What are you doing?"

Fred ran up to his brother. He was all out of breath, but smiling and curious.

Suddenly, a sharp yell cut through the air. Five Indians on horseback came

Billy took a long drink.

riding towards the buffalo. They had come to get fresh meat for their tribe.

The buffalo were frightened by the Indians' cry and began to run. And they were headed right towards Billy and Fred!

The boys dashed in the other direction. But the buffalo were getting closer and closer.

Then Fred tripped and fell. He screamed in pain. One leg was hurt badly.

Billy ran back and helped Fred to his feet. The boys tried to get away. But they were moving too slowly. The buffalo were almost on top of them.

Two of the Indians saw what was happening. They rode towards the boys and picked them up. Billy and Fred were safe!

At first, the boys were afraid of the Indians. But then the Indians smiled at

Two of the Indians rode towards the boys.

them. Billy and Fred grinned back. Together, they all rode back to the wagon train.

Everyone there was glad to see the boys. They had begun to worry when they realized the boys were gone.

The leader of the wagon train spoke sign language. He thanked the Indians and gave them some fresh fruit. The Indians tasted their first orange that day.

Then, in turn, the Indians gave the people of the wagon train some dried meat. This was the first buffalo meat that Billy and Fred ever had. It tasted salty and good at the same time.

Later, the Indians rode off. Billy and Fred waved good-bye. They knew the Indians had saved their lives.

And they knew something else, too. From now on, they would stay close to the wagon train.

The Bar-Q

Mike and Alan rode their horses past the Bar-Q Ranch.

"Hold on," Mike said. "I think something's wrong."

The two men rode towards the corral. Mr. Evans was leaning against the railing. His head was down and he stood completely still.

Mike and Alan rode towards the corral.

Mr. Evans owned the Bar-Q. He was an old man without much money. He tried to work his ranch by himself.

Once, he had been a famous horse trainer. But since he had come to Maggie Valley, he'd had nothing but bad luck.

Mike walked over to Mr. Evans. "Is everything all right?" he asked.

Mr. Evans looked up. He seemed sad, tired, and very old. "Rustlers came this morning," he said. "I haven't felt too well since then."

The old man told Mike and Alan that the rustlers had taken most of his horses. "I needed to sell those horses to meet my loan. I'm ruined."

"Were the horses branded?" Mike asked.

Mr. Evans shook his head. "I'm alone here. There just wasn't enough time."

Mike and Alan took Mr. Evans into his house. He told them that the gang of rustlers had been robbing him repeatedly for about a month.

"They've been here five times. I tried to get help. But no one offered."

"Do you have any horses left?" asked Mike.

"I have a few in the south pasture," Mr. Evans said.

"We'll bring them in," said Alan.

Mike and Alan took care of the horses. By that time, Mike had figured out a plan.

"We're going to brand them," he said, "but not the usual way."

Mike didn't brand the horses with a hot iron. Instead, he used a sharp knife. On the hoof of each horse, he carved a tiny line and a small Q.

"This shows that the horse belongs to

the Bar-Q," he said.

"But you can't see the brand unless you know it's there," said Alan.

"Exactly!" Mike smiled. "Now, we'll have to hope those rustlers come back for one more shot!"

Mike decided to stay with Mr. Evans at the ranch. Sure enough, three days later, the rustlers struck again!

"I hope this plan works," said Mike. "So far, so good."

Mike found Alan in town. Together, they went to the horse auction down by the railroad. Mike looked at all the horses. But none of them had the tiny Bar-Q brand.

He went to the auction every day for a week. None of the horses had the Bar-Q brand.

Then, one afternoon, two men came to the auction. They were strangers and had about thirty horses.

Mike went into the corral. He looked at one of the horses as though he might like to buy it. He felt the horse's leg. Then, down on the hoof, he saw what he was looking for – a tiny Bar-Q!

"Get the sheriff," Mike told Alan. Then, he walked over to the strangers.

"You've got some nice horses," he said.

"Do you want to buy any?" one of the strangers asked.

"I don't buy stolen goods," said Mike.

"Stolen goods?" the man laughed. "These horses don't even have a brand."

Now, it was Mike's turn to laugh. "We'll see about that," he said.

Alan and the sheriff came into the corral.

Mike showed them his tiny brand. The sheriff nodded to Mike. Then he pulled out his gun.

Mike showed them his tiny brand.

"We don't like rustlers," the sheriff told the strangers. "You boys had better come with me."

The sheriff told Mike he could take all of the horses with the Bar-Q brand.

"But what about the others?" Mike said. "I'm sure they belong to Mr. Evans!"

"Without proof, I can't let you have them," the sheriff said. "I'm sorry."

Mike and Alan took the horses back to the Bar-Q. Mike thought Mr. Evans would be upset. But he wasn't.

"You caught those crooks," Mr. Evans said. "That's the main thing."

"But what about your loan?" Mike said.

"Don't worry," Mr. Evans said. "I'll get by."

Mike and Alan were about to leave. But the sheriff rode up.

"I went through my wanted posters," he said with a grin. "You boys have a big reward coming."

The rustlers were wanted in three states. They had been at their trade for quite some time.

"I hope you can use $4,000," the sheriff smiled.

Mike ran into the house and told Mr. Evans the news.

"I want you to have some of the money," Mike said.

Mr. Evans shook his head. "That's mighty generous of you, Mike!" he said. "But I couldn't take any money. You caught those thieves."

"But they were your horses," Mike said.

Mr. Evans looked at Mike and Alan. He had an idea that would please everybody.

"I'll take that money," Mr. Evans said, "but on one condition."

"What?"

"That the three of us become partners," Mr. Evans said. "We'll share the ranch."

"Are you sure?" asked Mike. "Your ranch is worth more than that."

"Of course, I'm sure. You boys helped me when no one else would. Besides, I need some help around here."

Mike and Alan looked at each other. Then they looked at their new home.

"We'll call this place, the Bar-Q Plus 2," Mr. Evans said. Then, all three partners went into the house for a fresh pot of hot coffee.

The Wild Pony

In Montana, there's an old legend of the Wild Pony. It's said that, when the moon is full, the Wild Pony appears on Sapphire Mountain. It comes to look for its true master. And then, together, they ride into the sky and beyond.

The legend says that the Wild Pony has never found its true master. And

When the moon is full, the Wild Pony appears on Sapphire Mountain.

when the moon changes, the Wild Pony always leaves the mountain.

In Phillipsburg, Montana, two cowboys were talking about the legend.

"You believe that story, don't you?" Slim Jenkins asked his pal, Red Sweeny.

"You bet," Red said. "And we're going to find that Wild Pony."

"You're crazy," Slim said.

"Maybe," Red said. "And I just might be crazy enough to find that horse."

"Then, you'll have *two* horses," Slim said. Slim took a practical approach to things. Red, on the other hand, was a dreamer.

"Will you come with me to Sapphire Mountain?" Red asked.

Slim thought for a minute.

"I reckon I'll come along," he said. "It gets crazy in town, anyway, with a full moon."

As they rode towards Sapphire Mountain, Red sang while Slim played his mouth organ.

"Where are we going to look for this horse?" Slim asked after two days on the trail.

"I don't know yet," Red said. "I was hoping *it* would come to *me*."

Slim rolled his eyes. "You're a case, Red."

Red and Slim made their way up the mountain. They set up camp near a cliff. From there, they could see the valley below.

Red stayed awake that night. It was the first night of the full moon. He had a pair of binoculars. But he didn't see anything.

Three nights passed. Red had not seen even a rabbit or a fox. Slim thought it might be time to give up.

"Are you ready to go back to town and find some work?" Slim asked.

"We've still got two more nights of the full moon!" Red cried. "I can't leave yet."

But that night, Red still hadn't seen the Wild Pony.

When Slim woke up the next morning, he saw Red sitting by the fire.

"No luck?" Slim asked.

"Nope," answered Red. "Tonight's the last night. We'll head back tomorrow."

"Suits me," said Slim.

That night, the wind howled. Clouds moved across the sky and hid the moon.

Red had trouble staying awake. Once, he thought he heard the cry of a horse in the distance. Then, in the valley, Red thought he saw a form moving across the meadow.

But clouds hid the moon and Red couldn't see very well. Soon after that, he fell asleep.

Red dreamed about the Wild Pony. He dreamed that it had come to find him. He was the true master of the Wild Pony.

In Red's dream, the pony walked into camp. It stood over Red. But, as the moon grew dim, the Wild Pony disappeared.

Slim woke up first that morning. He found Red asleep near what was left of the fire. The fire had nearly died out.

"Hey," Slim yelled. "You can't see a thing with your eyes closed!"

Red bolted awake. He shook his head and rubbed his eyes.

"The Wild Pony was here!" he cried. But then, Red knew it had only been a dream.

"I fell asleep," Red said. "I dreamed that the Wild Pony walked into camp.

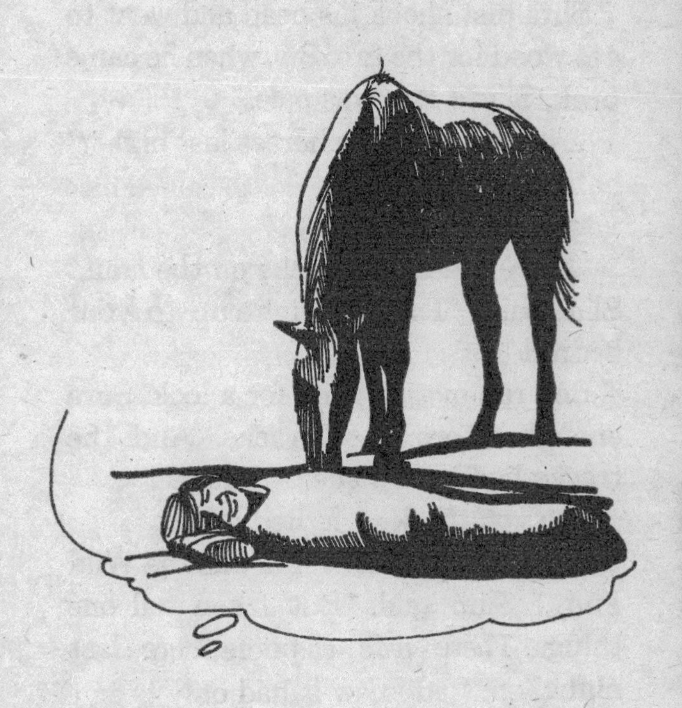

Red dreamed about the Wild Pony.

He stood right by my bedroll."

Slim just shook his head and went to get wood for the fire. But when he came back, Slim's face was pale.

"Did you untie the horses last night?" he asked.

"No," Red said. "Why?"

"There are horse tracks on the trail," Slim said. "They go right up to your bedroll."

Red ran over to Slim for a look. Sure enough, there were tracks. And the tracks had been made by a horse.

"Do you think . . . ?" Red asked.

"Now, I don't know if it was the Wild Pony," Slim said. "But I can tell one thing. There *was* a horse here last night."

Red looked into the valley for a long time.

"I'm coming back for the next full

moon," he said.

Slim nodded.

"And I'm coming with you," said Slim. "Except next time, I'm going to stay awake with you."

The Land Between the Lakes

"Ed, you just wouldn't understand," said Claire. "If I ever go to the Land Between the Lakes, I'm going alone."

Ed put down his guitar. He looked at Claire with a slow, steady gaze. "Why?" he asked.

Claire rose to her feet and looked

across the water. "I've just got to, that's all."

Ed moved towards Claire, but she stopped him.

"Ed, you're a good friend. But, how many times do we have to have this same talk? You know I don't feel about you the same way you feel about me."

"You might," Ed said. He had always had a special place in his heart for Claire. But she had always been restless and aloof.

Then she turned and smiled at him. "Will you play that song again?" she asked.

As Ed played, Claire stared across the water. She thought about the words to the song, and what they meant to her.

The song was about the Land Between the Lakes, near their home town. In fact, from her porch, Claire could see a hazy outline of the land across the water.

The song told the story of a young girl who saw a rainbow over the Land Between the Lakes. She crossed the water to follow the rainbow. And, at the end of the rainbow, she found her true love, in the Land Between the Lakes.

"I love that song," Claire said when Ed finished. "Who wrote it?"

"I don't know," Ed said. "Nobody knows. It's just a tune that's been handed down from picker to picker. It's more of a legend than anything else."

"Well, I think it's true. I *know* it's true," Claire said. "And when I see a rainbow over the Land Between the Lakes, I'm going to follow it."

"Well, be careful," Ed said. "That's wild country out there."

Claire stood up and yawned. "Thanks

for coming by, Ed," she said.

"Sure," Ed said. "See you." He walked down the path towards his cabin, leaving Claire alone in the moonlight.

A few days later, Claire was on her porch. She felt a sudden chill in the air. Dark clouds swirled in the western sky. Soon, thunder cracked, sending a hard rain.

Then, as quickly as the storm had formed, it stopped. The air grew misty and light. When the sun peeked through the clouds, Claire gasped.

Across the water, above the Land Between the Lakes, a rainbow glistened.

"Oh, my gosh," Claire said. The rainbow's end was in the heart of the Land Between the Lakes.

Claire ran down the trail to the edge of the water. She kept a small fishing boat in front of her house. The oars were lying

The rainbow's end was in the heart of the Land Between the Lakes.

inside the boat, and in just a few moments, she was on her way across the water.

As she rowed, she watched the rainbow. But when she reached the other side, the rainbow was gone.

Claire went into the forest. It was thick and overgrown. *Ed was right about it being wild,* she thought.

Claire thrashed her way farther and farther into the woods. It was hard to walk, but she kept going.

At last, she came to a small clearing. And in the middle of the clearing, a large rock rose high above the land.

She climbed the rock and stood on top to see where she was.

Somewhere behind her, a branch snapped. Claire turned towards the sound. She saw something move in the bushes.

Then, she heard a long, harsh growl. It sounded like a cat – a very big cat.

Claire panicked and tried to leap from the rock. But one foot slipped on the side of the rock. As she fell, she heard a bone crack.

Claire tried to stand, but she fell down again. Her heart began to pound when she heard the growl a second time. Trying to crawl, she looked back towards the bushes.

At first, she just saw its head. Then, she saw what it was – a huge mountain lion. It ran towards Claire and leaped into the air.

At the same instant, a rifle shot rang out. The lion fell just a few feet from Claire. It didn't move.

Someone moved into the clearing. It was Ed.

"Ed!" Claire gasped. "What are you

Then, Claire saw what it was—a huge mountain lion.

doing here?"

Ed nudged the lion to make sure it was dead. Then, he turned towards Claire.

"Well, I saw the rainbow. And I guessed you might come out here. When I saw your boat was gone, I came over."

Ed helped Claire get to her feet.

"Ouch," she winced. "I think my ankle may be broken."

"I'll get you home. Then, I'll go for Doc Brown."

"All right," Claire said. "Ed?"

"Yeah?"

"Thanks."

"Sure," Ed said. "I know I'm not what you were looking for out here. But I'll bet you're glad to see me."

"I am," Claire said. "I am."

She held his arm tighter as they left the Land Between the Lakes.

The Long Way Home

Sally and Beth lived near a desert. They loved to explore the land near their home. Often they took their ponies and their dog, Scotty, and rode into the desert.

Their father had made a trail with signs. That way, they wouldn't get lost.

One day, Sally and Beth were sitting at home.

"Why can't we go?" Sally asked her father.

"It looks like a storm is heading our way," he said. "I want you both to stay here!"

Their father meant what he said. Years ago, their mother had died in a desert storm.

The girls looked out their window. There were just a few clouds in the sky.

And when their father rode to town, Sally and Beth went out to the barn. They saddled their ponies and rode into the desert. Scotty followed them.

The girls had been riding for an hour, when they came to a tall cactus. The cactus marked the end of their father's trail.

"Let's go farther!" Sally called to her sister. "As long as we can see the cactus, we'll be all right."

"Let's go farther!" Sally called to her sister.

At first, Beth was reluctant. But when Sally rode away, Beth went, too. She didn't want to be stranded alone in the desert!

The girls rode for a long time. Soon, Scotty was panting and out of breath. The horses were tired, too.

After a while, they stopped for lunch. They had brought sandwiches. And they had a canteen filled with cool, spring water.

But as they were eating, the wind began to gust. Suddenly, a sandstorm was upon them!

A desert sandstorm happens quickly. It strikes as fast as a rattlesnake. And it can be just as deadly!

The horses were wild with fear. They broke their reins and started running!

Sally, Beth, and Scotty lay on the ground, waiting for the storm to pass.

Sometimes, a sandstorm lasts for hours. Sometimes, it lasts just long enough to hide a trail. That's what happened this time. The storm stopped, but now their trail was covered.

Sally stood up. She looked for the cactus. But they had ridden too far. Now, Sally and Beth were lost!

Beth began to cry.

"It's going to be all right," Sally said. But the sun was very hot. And they were a long way from home.

"We'd better start walking," said Sally.

"Which way?" Beth asked.

Sally just took a guess. "This way," she said. "We'll see the cactus soon!"

They had to walk slowly because of the heat. They kept looking for the cactus. But they couldn't see it.

"It'll be dark soon," Sally said. "We'd

better find a place to stay for the night."

Beth started crying again. Scotty ran over to her and placed a paw on her knee.

Then Sally saw some boulders. "We'll stay there," she said. Sally and Beth sat near the rocks. They watched the sun dip slowly out of sight.

As darkness fell, it became cold. Scotty came over to the girls. And the three of them kept each other warm. Finally, they fell asleep.

In the morning, they were thirsty and hungry. But there was nothing left to eat or drink.

"We've got to get home!" Sally said. "Come on."

"Are we going the right way?" her sister asked.

"We'd better be," Sally said. She knew

They watched the sun dip slowly out of sight.

they couldn't last very long without water.

They walked for a long time. Sally and Beth grew dizzy from the heat.

Then, in the distance, Sally saw a welcome sight!

It was the tall cactus! Scotty barked. They *were* on the right way home. But they had been very lucky!

Sally and Beth felt hot and weak. But they kept going. Finally, they saw their home.

Their father was standing on the porch with a group of men. As soon as he saw the girls, he ran out to meet them.

"Thank goodness!" he cried. Then, he became angry. "I told you not to go out there!" he yelled. "We were coming to look for you."

Finally, they saw their home.

"It was my fault," Sally said. "I just didn't want to listen."

She hugged her father. "But you don't have to worry anymore," she said. "We won't be doing dumb things like that ever again!"

A Ranger In Waco

Louie Blake threw his frying pan towards the wall. He kicked his work-table and threw a batch of carrots out the window. He tore off his apron and stomped on it with his feet.

Then he yelled. "I've had it. I won't chop anymore. I won't peel, and I never want to fry again!"

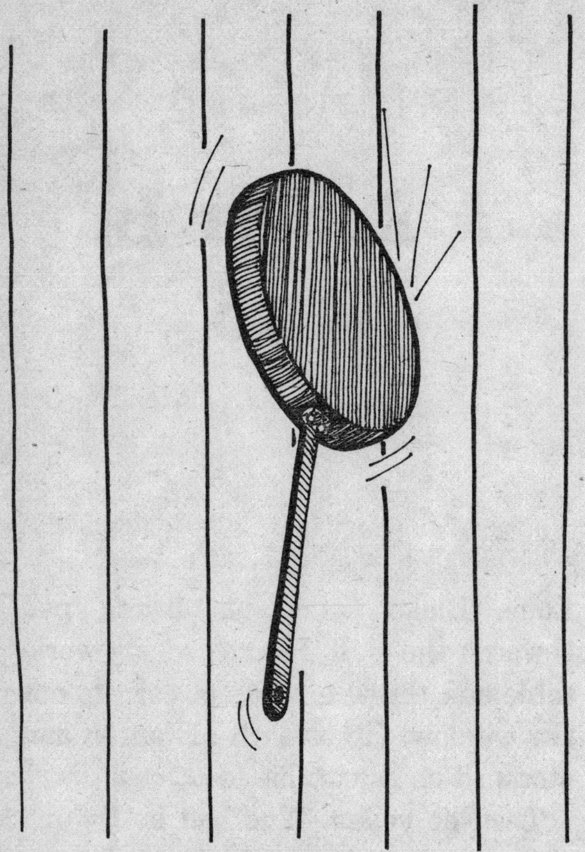

Louie threw his frying pan towards the wall.

Louie was the cook's helper at the Full Moon Ranch. And he had lost his temper plenty of times in the past. Luke, the head cook, would calm him down. But today was different.

Louie meant to quit. And he did just that.

Luke was shocked when his helper came back to the kitchen with his bag packed. "You're really going, aren't you?" he asked.

"Yeah," said Louie. "I want to see what else I can do besides cook."

"But you're getting to be a good cook," Luke said.

"Maybe I am. But I'm sick of it. Cooking just doesn't have any zing to it. I want to do things I can be proud of. I'm going to be a Texas Ranger."

"Are you sure about that, Louie?"

"Luke, my mind is made up. I'm going

to Waco."

It took Louie three days to reach Waco. When he got into town, he bought a new outfit. He looked just fine in his new vest, chaps, jeans, and boots. But he walked a little stiff.

Louie liked his new clothes and felt like a ranger already. He'd never ridden a wild horse before, but now he was determined to try.

Riding broncos sure has zing, he thought.

Louie put his bag in the bunkhouse. Then he told the camp captain what he wanted to do.

"We expect all of our new rangers to train their own horses," the captain said.

"That suits me," said Louie.

When he got to the corral, a ranger handed him a rope. "Go choose a horse and train it," the ranger said.

There were five horses in the corral. Louie hadn't had much experience with broncos. But these seemed tame.

He chose a small gray mare. She looked like she wouldn't be too tough to ride.

But Louie soon found out he was wrong.

When he tried to toss a loop around the mare's neck, she moved out of the way just at the right moment. He tried a few more times. But each time, the mare dodged the rope.

Louie chased her around the corral for a while. When he stopped to rest, the mare looked at him with a twinkle in her eyes.

A crowd began to gather at the corral. It was fun to watch a new guy try to ride a bronco.

Soon, the whole camp was watching. They tried not to laugh at first. But the mare was having so much fun with Louie, the rangers couldn't help themselves.

The more they laughed, the harder Louie tried. But the mare kept prancing away from him.

Finally, Louie walked up to the horse and looked her in the eyes.

"This rope is for you," he said. "Then I'm going to ride."

He tossed the loop around the horse's neck. And the whole camp cheered. But in an instant, Louie wished he had missed again.

The mare reared high into the air. Louie held on tight to the rope. Then she raced around the corral. When he fell down, at last, the mare dragged him through the dust.

Louie finally let go of the rope. While the whole camp laughed at him, he left the corral. His face was red with shame.

It looks like I'm not cut out to be a ranger, he thought. *I can't even rope a horse, much less ride one.*

Louie trudged back towards the bunkhouse. He heard a lot of yelling coming from a tent along the way. So, he went to see what was going on.

Inside the tent, a few rangers were throwing rolls at the camp cook. The cook was hiding behind a chair. But now and then, a roll hit him, and he moaned in pain. When they were out of rolls, the rangers stormed out.

"You're in for it, if you don't give us a good meal soon," one of the rangers yelled.

Louie picked up one of the rolls. It was as hard as a rock.

"You can't blame them," he said to the cook. "This isn't food. It's a weapon."

The cook was hiding behind a chair.

The roll thudded when Louie tossed it onto the table.

"What am I going to do?" the cook said. "I didn't want this job. But I was the only one who would try. Now, I haven't got a friend in camp."

"That makes two of us," said Louie. "The whole camp saw me make a fool of myself today. Listen, how about if I give you a hand? I've done some cooking."

"That'd be great!" The cook held his hand out to Louie. "I'm called Taco. It was the only thing the boys almost ate."

"I'm Louie, and I'm glad to meet you. Now, let's get to it."

Louie and Taco worked all afternoon. They made beef stew with a tangy sauce. They baked bread. And they cooked vegetables.

At last, they put the food in the dining room and waited for the rangers.

"We'd better stay in the kitchen," Taco said. "If they don't like the food, they get pretty riled up."

The rangers came in to eat. There was a hush in the room at first. They looked at the food on the table. It didn't look like the stuff Taco had made before. And when they tasted it, they all talked at once.

"Say, this stuff is great!"

"Did *Taco* do this?"

"This is a great meal!"

The rangers were happy. And Louie was glad to have helped Taco get through the meal. He started to leave.

"Hold on a minute," Taco said. "Come with me."

Taco went into the dining room. The camp cheered. Taco was the camp's new hero.

"Hold it, boys," he said. "You're cheering for the wrong man. This is Louie. You must have seen him down at the corral today."

The rangers laughed.

"Well, he may not be too much of a bronco rider," Taco went on, "but he sure can cook. He's the one who fixed all this food."

The camp cheered again. Some of the rangers shook Louie's hand.

"I think we ought to make Louie the head chef of the Texas Rangers. What do you say, boys?"

The camp roared with approval. Then the camp captain stood up.

"I think we've got our cook at last," he said. "How about it, Louie?"

"Sure, I'll be glad to be head cook," said Louie, smiling. "I guess I wanted to be a ranger—you know, ride the broncos and yell a lot. But you boys make me

He put away his boots, vest, and chaps for good.

feel that cooking is a big deal. I guess there's some zing to cooking after all."

Louie made a lot of friends among the Texas Rangers. And he didn't mind that he'd put away his boots, vest, and chaps for good.